PAIR-IT BOOKS™

Bo Peep's Sheep

Written by Gare Thompson

Illustrated by Éva Vágréti Cockrille

STECK-VAUGHN
C O M P A N Y
ELEMENTARY • SECONDARY • ADULT • LIBRARY

Little Bo Peep looks for her sheep.

Little Bo Peep looks left.

Little Bo Peep looks right.

Little Bo Peep looks up.

Little Bo Peep looks down.

Little Bo Peep looks all around.

The sheep find Little Bo Peep.